For Joshua, of course – M.D.
For Erin – K.W-M.

Text copyright © 2004 Malachy Doyle
Illustrations copyright © 2004 Ken Wilson-Max

Published by Bloomsbury, New York and London
Distributed to the trade by Holtzbrinck Publishers

Library of Congress Cataloging-in-Publication Data
Doyle, Malachy. Splash, Joshua, splash! / Malachy Doyle ; illustrated by Ken Wilson-Max. p. cm
Summary: Joshua enjoys water splashing when he feeds the ducks, walks his dog,
and especially when he and his grandmother splash in the swimming pool.
ISBN: 1-58234-837-5 (alk paper)
[1. Grandmothers—Fiction. 2. Water—Fiction.] I. Wilson-Max, Ken, ill. II. Title.
PZ7.D775SP2004   [E]—dc22   2003056253

Designed by Manya Stojic @ Pumpkin Ideas for Children

Printed in Hong Kong/China

1 3 5 7 9 10 8 6 4 2

Bloomsbury USA Children's Books
175 Fifth Avenue
New York, New York 10010

All papers used by Bloomsbury Publishing are natural, recyclable products
made from wood grown in sustainable, well-managed forests.
The manufacturing processes conform to the environmental regulations of the country of origin.

Splash, Joshua, Splash!

Malachy Doyle

illustrated by
Ken Wilson - Max

BLOOMSBURY
CHILDREN'S
BOOKS

Joshua Joshua's down by the river,

Joshua Joshua's feeding the ducks.

Joshua's throwing the bread in the water,

"Splash!" says Joshua.

"Splash!"

Joshua Joshua's out in the country,
Joshua Joshua's walking the dog.
Joshua's jumping in all of the puddles,
"Splash!" says Joshua. "Splash!"

Joshua's Granny is doing her shopping,
Joshua's doing his shopping as well.

Joshua's trying to climb in the fountain,
"Splash!" says Joshua Joshua.

Joshua's Granny is wearing her swimsuit,
Joshua's wearing his swimming trunks, too.
Granny is shivering. Joshua's quivering,
"Splash!" says Joshua. "Splash!"

Joshua Joshua's leading his Granny
up to the top of the Gigantic Slide.
"What happens now?"
asks Joshua's
Granny.

"Splash!"
says Joshua Joshua.

Round and round goes Joshua's Granny,

"Wheee!" says Joshua,

"Wheee!" says Joshua,

faster and faster and...

SPLASH!

Deep down, under the water,
under the water, deep down.
Into the froth and the foam,
and the bubbles,
splashing and crashing,
fizzing and sparkling.

Up, up, back to the surface,
dripping and blinking
and looking for Granny . . .
who's laughing!

**Who's dripping and blinking
and looking at Joshua ...
laughing!**

"More!" says Joshua, whooping and yelling,
"More!" says Joshua.
"More, more!"

So up they climb, and down they sail, and **SPLASH!** they crash, into the water.

Up they climb, and down they sail, and **SPLASH!** they crash, again and again.

Now Joshua's on the way home
with his Grandmother,
slumbering home on the number nine bus.
Splash! go the wheels,
through the rain-sodden streets,
but Joshua and Granny
are too tired to see.

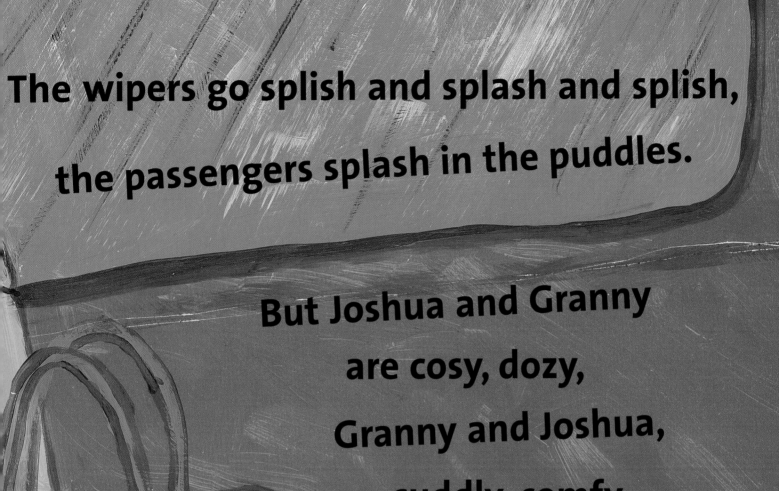

The wipers go splish and splash and splish,

the passengers splash in the puddles.

But Joshua and Granny

are cosy, dozy,

Granny and Joshua,

cuddly, comfy,

Joshua and Granny

are snuggled up close,

in a huddle-up, cuddle-up,

snooze.